Copyright © 2022 E S Monk

Published 2022

ISBN 9798413870501

Hollybrook Stables

Winters Rescue

By

E.S. Monk

For

Michelle

Clare

Clare turned to face the back of the church once the string quartet struck up and began to play the wedding march. She watched the heavy oak church door open and there was Suzie, the picture of radiance, gliding up the aisle wearing her elegant long-sleeved, ivory-coloured satin dress being escorted by her two sons, John and Joseph. The boys were smiling broadly, handsome and proud in their miniature top hats and tails.

The entire church was bursting with autumnal blooms. Every nook and cranny of the quaint little church was overflowing with artistic displays of seasonal flowers in reds and golds and dusty orange. As the weak sun shone through the multi-coloured stained-glass windows, it cast a warm glow upon the joyous gathering.

Clare felt her eyes fill with happy tears, looking at Luke, tall and handsome in his wedding suit. He watched his bride to be walk towards him. *Such a wonderful couple,* she thought, seeing them standing side by side at the altar.

The crowd cheered once the vicar pronounced Suzie and Luke to be man and wife, permitting Luke to embrace his new bride and share the first kiss of their marriage. Taking Suzie's hand, Luke led her down the aisle amidst the smiles, congratulatory hugs and handshakes from all their friends.

Clare slipped out of the side door of the church straight after the kiss took place, to meet Rose and help with the surprise they had secretly planned for the happy couple and their guests.

"Quick, come and take Clarissa, she's eating the flower display in the entrance way," Rose called out as soon as she saw her.

Taking control of the wayward pony, Clare positioned herself and Clarissa next to Rose and Gilly. Both horses had been bathed and groomed to perfection the day before, then secured in their stables overnight to ensure they remained immaculate for the wedding. Clare, Rose, Ellen, Riley and Jem had painstakingly prepared the patient horses early that morning. Autumnal coloured ribbons were braided into their manes and tails, their hooves were sparkling with hoof polish and a wreath of seasonal flowers hung around each of their necks.

Joe, Molly, Matthew, David, Ben, and Noah had been drafted into the secret as tack cleaners. Both saddles and bridles were polished and buffed to perfection, and carefully draped over the saddles were beautifully hand-crafted leather saddle bags, with the names of Suzie and Luke engraved in gold letters on the corner of one, and John and Joseph on the other. A wedding gift from them all, for the picnics Suzie, Luke and the boys would be taking in the future, and a happy reminder of the picnic where the proposal had taken place. But, for now, the saddle bags were filled to the brim with chocolates and treats for all the guests to help themselves to on exiting the church.

All the hard work was worth it when Clare saw the look of surprise, swiftly followed by delight on Suzie and Luke's faces when they stepped outside the church and were greeted by the smart horses.

"Clarissa, Gilly, you look fantastic," exclaimed Suzie, going straight up to Clarissa and kissing her nose. She turned to Clare. "What a wonderful surprise to have our horses here on our special day!" she said. "Thank you."

"Everyone helped," replied Clare, gesturing towards the Hollybrook gang. "We all agreed that Clarissa and Gilly should be part of your day."

After twenty minutes of photographs with the beautifully turned-out horses in front of the church, and when everyone had enjoyed their fill of treats, Clare and Rose announced that they must take the horses home, as the wedding party was soon to begin!

Laughing and waving to the remaining guests, they headed back to Hollybrook stables to prepare for the bride and groom's arrival at the wedding reception.

Rose

The day before the wedding had not been a good day. Rose knew it was coming. Hubert's owner, Grace, and herself had discussed many times over the previous months that when the time was right, she would know, and to call Rose immediately.

And the time was yesterday morning. At nine on the dot, she received the call, and between the heartbroken woman's tears, she arranged to meet Grace and Hubert at midday. Rose had known Hubert for fifteen years. He had been one her first clients as a newly qualified vet. He was a miniature chestnut Shetland gelding with a flaxen mane and tail, and the apple of his owner's eye. Grace had suffered with empty nest syndrome twenty years ago when her second and youngest daughter moved out of home. Her husband was still working full time and Grace found herself idling away long lonely days without her daughters to care for and a husband only needing his supper prepared and shirts ironed. House chores she did contentedly, but it was not enough without her girls to fully occupy her time. She came across Hubert when a friend explained that she was having to rehome the dear little thing because her children just weren't interested in the pony. On a whim, and not knowing anything about horses, Grace said she would take him, and for the next twenty years, Grace and little Hubert were the best of friends, enjoying hours of long grooming sessions and adventurous walks around the countryside together, and when her husband finally retired, he accompanied them. Hubert had very much filled the void when her girls left home. And now it was time for Grace to say goodbye.

Rose felt a lump forming in her throat before she even arrived. Little Hubert was now thirty-five, a grand old age for a pony, and all testament to the love and attention that Grace had bestowed on him for twenty years. But his time had come, and it wasn't fair on the little chap to suffer in pain from his rickety joints anymore. That morning, Grace had witnessed Hubert struggling desperately to get up. He managed it, but only just, and she would not let her darling boy suffer. It was the right thing for Hubert.

Grace held her dearest friend in her arms and whispered her goodbyes in his ears as Rose administered the injection to send him into a peaceful sleep, a sleep where he would feel no more pain, and a sleep that he would not wake up from.

It was a heart-breaking day for Grace and her husband, and a devastating day for Rose, too. Rose loved the adorable little pony. He never gave her any trouble, no matter what ailment she needed to treat. His easy-going temperament and clear idolization of his mistress made him a pleasure to be around over the many years of being his vet.

Rose excused herself quietly and left the grieving Grace with her equally emotionally broken husband. As soon as Rose reached the privacy and safety of her car, she broke down and wept. She loved her job, and she was proud of the hard work it had taken for her to achieve the ultimate ambition of her career, running her own practice. But on days like today, she just needed to break down and cry. Her job was both physically and mentally exhausting, and she had dedicated her entire life to getting the best grades at school, graduating veterinary school at the top of her class, and working her socks off to then learn everything you can't learn in school, through hands on experience, as a junior vet. Now at forty-one, she was feeling tired. She wasn't as robust as she used to be, and witnessing yet another owner lose their best friend wasn't so easy to shake off.

Things were so busy and chaotic on the morning of the wedding, that she was able to forget about her terrible day and focus on Suzie and Luke and help prepare the horses. The wedding was as blissful as any wedding could be, and Rose, pleasantly relaxed, sat back in her chair, sipped her glass of champagne, and surveyed the warmth and happiness encased in the autumnal-themed decorated marquee at Hollybrook stables. *How lucky I am to have such lovely friends. Alas, I am all work and no play,* she thought wryly to herself. *Maybe it's time I had a mini-break?*

Riley

Riley was exhausted after a particularly energetic dance number with her boyfriend, Joe. She slipped away to top up her glass of champagne and enjoy a much needed five minutes rest. Sitting down, she put her aching feet up on the empty chair next to her and smiled as she watched Joe spinning Molly on the dance floor.

What a wonderful day, she thought, looking at all the merry people surrounding her, and Suzie and Luke dancing wildly together, having the time of their lives celebrating the beginning of their marriage.

Riley began to feel an unwelcome dull ache in the pit of her belly, a feeling that was becoming more and more frequent since arriving home from Australia and receiving a letter from Nell, her mother. She knew it by heart, but after four months, she still hadn't been able to reply. She simply didn't know how to respond.

Dear Riley

I was so pleased to hear from my friend in the village that you, Joe and Molly arrived home safely. I'm sorry it has taken me so long to write, I have been focusing on getting better. I didn't want to contact you until I knew I would be able to offer you and Molly consistency and honesty. A lot has happened in the twelve months since I last saw you, and I have been sober now for eleven months. I completed my rehab program and continue to attend my meetings. I have a small but lovely flat and also a job as a shop assistant, and I've made some new friends. I'm sorry, Riley. I'm sorry for everything that I put you through. I would very much like to see you if you would like to see me. Molly too, of course. I will be ready and waiting for whenever that time might be.

Love Mum x

Joe had been great, explaining that he would support her with whatever decision she made. Clare also offered her support with whatever she decided upon but said that she should think carefully about what to do next. The letter showed that her mother was acknowledging the impact of her behaviour, at last, and taking responsibility for it. Maybe she had changed? Maybe she wanted to right the wrongs she had done to Riley and Molly? Maybe Riley would be able to move on if she met with her mother, even if it was just the once? Clare's reply had given Riley a lot to think about.

The wedding was filled with a sense of intoxicating elation, and as she watched all the happy families together, Riley wished that her family had been a happy one. *Could my family be like that?* she asked herself. *Now that she's sober, could I trust her not to hurt me and Molly like she has done so many times before?*

Molly and Joe were waving madly at her, beckoning her to join them on the dance floor. *Thinking time is over,* she mused. *Well, for now anyway.* She pushed her way through the throng of dancing bodies to join Molly and Joe.

Jem

Jem was settled on a comfy chair in a quiet, darkened corner of the raucous wedding reception cradling six-week-old baby Tilly. Although the party was still in full swing, she was absolutely worn out and ready to go home. Not wanting to ruin Ben and Noah's fun, she called a taxi before telling Ben she was leaving. That way, he wouldn't feel that they had to leave the party with her. Truth be told, she just wanted to be on her own and spend some time alone with Tilly.

Everyone wanted to meet Tilly as soon as they possibly could after they both arrived home from hospital. That, with the build up to Suzie's wedding, meant that she and Tilly had spent very little alone time together, so tonight, she was going to do what she wanted, and that was to have a cuddle with her baby girl in peace.

Jem welcomed the silence as she stepped into her home. "Finally, peace and quiet," she whispered to the sleeping Tilly. Kicking her shoes off, she settled on the sofa and cried. Alone, in the privacy of her own home, she could finally let it all out. Ever since Tilly was born, all she wanted to do was bury herself under her duvet and give way to her tears. It all just seemed too much. Everything felt like it was piling up on top of her and she just couldn't see a way out of it.

Jem, Ben and Noah had been so excited about the impending arrival of the baby. They had decorated the nursery and prepared everything as a family, and Jem had never felt so happy. And then she arrived, a beautiful daughter, a sister for Noah, and since then she had felt nothing but misery and desperation. The words just swirled round and round in her head. *I'm not good enough, I'm not a good partner to Ben, I'm not a good mother, I'm doing everything wrong, I don't know how to be better.*

She felt like she was on a carousel. Round and round she went, with no way off.

Ben had tentatively mentioned that he thought she was feeling a bit down and suggested that they speak to the midwife. Jem agreed, and the midwife explained about the baby blues. She'd assured her that she would feel better in a day or two, but that was three weeks ago. She tried to think back to when Noah was born. She didn't ever remember feeling anything but pride and joy. She'd wanted to show him off to anyone and everyone. With Tilly, all she wanted to do was be at home, away from the world, and under her duvet.

The jubilation-filled wedding party had simply overwhelmed her, and she had felt anxiety flooding through her during the evening, until eventually she was able to return to the solitary sanctuary of her own home. But now, alone with the silence of the house oppressing her, she felt nothing but a growing sense of hopelessness.

Suzie

"Are you ready, ladies?" Suzie called out, turning away from the collection of single women who had gathered around her. With one almighty throw, she launched her bouquet over her head, far over the gaggle of giggling girls, and it landed firmly on Rose's lap, the only single lady not in the crowd.

"Ooooooh!" exclaimed the onlookers, clapping and cheering in delight at the unexpected recipient.

Suzie skipped over to Rose, her arms outstretched, inviting her in for a friendly hug. When Rose stood to accept her embrace, she squeezed her tightly and whispered, "I so hoped it would be you. It's definitely your turn to find some happiness."

Rose gave her a bashful smile, and replied, "I hope you and Luke have enjoyed your day. Congratulations."

"Suzie and Luke, where are you? It's time to cut the cake," Clare called out over the hubbub of the wedding guests. Leaving Rose with her prize, Suzie scooped up the train of her dress and headed towards her cake. It was a three-tiered, perfectly iced, ivory-coloured cake, adorned with red, gold and orange flowers. The petals were as delicate as lace, and the bride and groom, mounted on horses identical to Clarissa and Gilly, took centre stage on the top tier.

Luke slipped one arm behind her and rested his hand on her hip, then placed the other on top of her hand. They gripped the knife together and sliced the first slice of their special cake, to the sound of cheering and clapping from their friends and family.

Suzie turned to face Luke. "Today has been the most spectacular day," she gushed, then reaching up on her tiptoes, she planted a kiss on his lips.

"You looked truly exquisite walking down the aisle in the church," said Luke. "My beautiful wife." And he picked her up off the ground and spun her round and round, the train of her dress swishing as she went.

"Your taxi will be here in ten minutes," Riley told them. "You'd better go and get ready! Your honeymoon awaits!"

Suzie and Luke had agreed at the beginning that it wasn't a traditional honeymoon they would be going on. The wedding was not just a union between Suzie and Luke, but the creation of a new family unit. Luke would officially become a member of John and Joseph's family and they both thought that the boys should accompany them on their trip. The holiday was to be the first of many family holidays and they wanted to celebrate their marriage as a family. The destination and activities had all been chosen together, and they'd all unanimously agreed on Thailand as their destination. They'd booked a family villa, situated on the golden sands, where relaxing spa treatments were available, as well as exciting water sports for them all to take part in. There was even a children's club, so that the boys could play with other children, allowing Suzie and Luke some time alone. The cherry on top was the option to visit the elephant sanctuary, situated within walking distance from their villa. It was a place where they could see and learn all about the exotic Asian elephant, and it was even possible to dine on the open terrace at sunset, overlooking the lake, where the elephants bathed every evening. They all agreed - the elephants would be the highlight of their trip.

Before long, Suzie, Luke, John and Joseph were all settled in the taxi, chatting animatedly about the exciting adventure they were about to embark on. Luke squeezed Suzie's hand and smiled at her, and zing...went her body. Her handsome husband never failed to set off the fireworks inside her with his winning smile, kindness and charismatic personality. Nestled in her cocoon, with her family all around her, Suzie had never felt so happy.

Clare

"What a day," Clare said, kicking off her heels and flopping down on the sofa.

"Cup of tea?" Asked her partner, Matthew, already on his way into the kitchen.

"Always," replied Clare.

The hectic six months of planning and preparations for the wedding all seemed worth it after waving Suzie, Luke, John and Joseph off in the taxi for their honeymoon. Every single person at the wedding told her that it was the best wedding they had ever been too. Everyone thought that Gilly and Clarissa offering treats outside the church was so original, that Suzie's dress was exquisite, and that the church decorations and the reception had all been perfect. It would be years before anyone could compete with such a wedding. The day had been a roaring success.

Matthew returned with their cups of tea and settled down on the sofa next to her. "Bags packed? Passport ready?" he asked her.

"I've been packed and ready for a week," Clare laughed in reply. "With everything going on with the wedding, I thought it best to be organised and have everything ready before the chaotic week of final wedding preparations got underway!"

Matthew couldn't believe it when Clare admitted that she had only ever been abroad twice, and both times to France. Once was with her parents, the only family trip they had taken abroad. The horses made holidays difficult, plus they never really felt the need to leave Hollybrook. They were content at home, together, with the horses. Clare remembered their trip with fondness. Being inexperienced travellers, her parents chose to take the ferry from Plymouth to Roscoff and hire a little holiday cottage in a neighbouring town. The four days were spent eating delicious French food and playing together on the pretty beach in the sunshine. Clare had loved every minute of it but was equally glad to return home and be back with her horses. Her second trip was a trip to France with school. They'd taken the train to London, then Eurostar to Paris. The highlights of the trip had been more delicious French food and a trip to the Eiffel tower. And that was the extent of her travel experience.

On hearing that Clare had been keen to travel in her younger days, before the loss of her parents and the somewhat unexpected arrival of baby Joe, Matthew asked her if she still had an interest in travel. He flew all over the world regularly for work, and he wanted Clare to experience some of the wonderful sights he enjoyed so much, if she still had an appetite for seeing the world.

Clare had mulled the idea over for days. Could she leave Hollybrook? *Joe and Riley were home now, would they agree to take charge whilst she was away?*

Her decision was made when Suzie excitedly announced her impending trip to Thailand. *How wonderfully exotic,* Clare thought, the idea of gallivanting around unknown lands quickly becoming appealing. And after discussing things with Joe and Riley, who both agreed she should go, she finally gave her decision to Matthew.

Two months, two whole months, accompanying Matthew to Spain, Austria, and Dubai for work. Matthew had also organised a week in Florence and a week in Greece, in between work destinations, so they could both relax, explore and immerse themselves in the culture and cuisine of both countries. Their taxi was booked for five in the morning to take them to the airport, and they would not return until Christmas Eve. Clare was beyond excited for the adventure she was about to undertake with Matthew.

Rose

Apart from the brief interlude of positivity and happiness with her friends at Suzie's wedding last week, Rose felt that life was as dire as ever. Monday morning brought her a dead cat. Some poor soul had accidently run it over, and they brought it to the surgery, asking if she could please deal with the body and check if it was microchipped so that the owner could be contacted. The little creature was indeed a very much-loved pet, but after dropping the cat off, the driver never returned, leaving Rose to contact the owner and break the devastating news about their little boy's beloved pet cat.

Threes, they always come in threes, Rose grumbled to herself, when she opened her emails on Tuesday morning to receive some very bad news. Ellen had asked her to do a veterinary check on a gorgeous horse that she wanted to buy, but its blood was laced with drugs, no doubt to curb unruly behaviour or mask some other hidden ailment that would require further investigation. Rose sighed.

More bad news to give, she thought, gathering her handbag and vet's case. *I'll pop into Hollybrook and see Ellen now. I might as well get it over and done with.*

Rose saw the disappointment in Ellen's face as she relayed the test results too her. "I'm so sorry Ellen, but I have to tell you that in my professional opinion, I do not recommend you buy that horse."

"Thanks Rose," Ellen replied. "I appreciate you coming to tell me, and highly value your opinion. I'll call the owners and let them know. Back to the drawing board then!" Ellen paused and looked at her with concern in her eyes, "Are you ok Rose? I hope you don't mind me saying, but you don't look too good."

Rose didn't really feel too good. The week of delivering bad news had taken its toll, along with the sheer volume of work she insisted on taking on. The local town veterinary centre frequently offered to help with her case load with their constant stream of junior vets desperate for work, but she struggled to deny her clients and their animals her own dedicated professional service.

Ellen's kindness, and her own sheer exhaustion, led her momentarily to break down. A brief burst of tears, swiftly followed by a firm word with herself - *pull yourself together* - she looked at Ellen and replied, "No, not really, I'm having a bit of a bad week."

Ellen sat down on a bale of hay in the yard and gestured for Rose to join her.

"Do you want to talk about it?"

Sitting down next to Ellen, the short emotional outburst appeared to be just the beginning, and between unrelenting bouts of sobbing, Rose stuttered out, as best she could, her overwhelming feelings of sadness that she just didn't seem to be able to shake off.

Ellen sat quietly with her and listened. When Rose had exhausted all her tears, and dried her eyes with her sleeve, Ellen announced, "You're doing too much, Rose. I think you need a break. If you carry on like this, you'll burn yourself out."

Rose just nodded silently, grateful to have finally confided in a friend.

"I think you should contact the vets in town and ask them to cover your clients whilst you take a few days off," Ellen continued. "And then on your return, discuss with them how you can share your workload with them."

Rose nodded again, knowing that it made sense, and if it were the other way round, she would be offering the same advice.

In a small voice, she replied, "You're right, Ellen. I need to do something about it now. What if I had broken down like this in front of a client? I would have died of embarrassment and been furious with myself for lack of professionalism, and that would have made me feel even worse. I think this...episode...for want of a better word, has been brewing for a while now."

Ellen smiled at her. "I'm here to talk whenever you need me."

"Thank you, Ellen," Rose replied. "You're a good friend. But what about you? I'm so sorry about the horse."

"Oh, don't worry about that. What's meant to be will be, and that horse clearly wasn't the one. With David's help, I'll find the right horse for me eventually."

"And when you find the one, I'll do the veterinary check for you again, hopefully with better results next time," Rose said with a rueful smile.

After a moment of comfortable silence between the two friends, Rose looked at her watch. "I have to go to my next client now, but thank you, I'm feeling much better," she gratefully told Ellen.

Riley

Riley was sitting on the bench outside the shop in town where her mother now worked. After the wedding, and a long talk with Joe, she felt the time was right, and she had replied to her mother's letter. A response arrived two days later stating that Nell would love to meet with her at her chosen date and time. Riley explained in her letter that it would be only her who her mother would see. She would not be disrupting Molly's life, and until Riley knew for sure that she was telling the truth, she would not be seeing Molly. Nell accepted her terms, and today, for the first time in sixteen months, she would be seeing her mum.

Riley noticed the change in her as soon as she saw her. Her clothes were clean and freshly pressed, her hair was cut and styled, and her make up subtle. A vast contrast to the overly made-up, scantily clad train wreck her mother used to be. Her persona was different too, calm, reserved and unintimidating. Not the woman Riley grew up with.

"Hello Riley," said Nell, hovering next to her, unsure what to do next.

"Hi, Mum," Riley replied, gesturing for her sit on the bench next to her.

Her mother offered Riley a paper bag, breaking the awkward tension between them. "I bought you this on my lunch break, they used to be your favourite."

Riley opened the bag to find a chocolate brownie inside. *Still my favourite,* she thought, touched and surprised at the gesture, and the fact that her mother even knew what her favourite treat was.

"I'd like to apologise to you, Riley," Nell said quietly. "I know I have many things to apologise for, but I think I need to start with Jerry first. I'm sorry for not protecting you from him. I'm sorry I let him into our home. My behaviour was unforgivable. For a mother to put her daughter in a situation like that and allow a man to behave like that and do nothing about it is inexcusable."

Riley felt a lump form in her throat on hearing the words she had so desperately wanted to hear for such a long time. But anger also simmered up inside her about what her mother did let Jerry do, and the thought that if Riley hadn't taken Molly away, what he might have done to her.

Molly wasn't like her. Molly was quiet and shy, and Riley shuddered to think what he might have done to her. She didn't think Molly would have been able defend herself and escape like she had done.

Riley needed time to think. "Thank you for the brownie, I have to go now Mum," she said, standing up and facing her mother.

"Ok, thank you for listening," replied Nell, pushing a piece of paper into her hand. "My phone number, if you'd like it? Not for phone calls," she stammered. "But maybe messages? It might be easier to communicate that way rather than letters. Anyway, it's your choice, Riley. Hopefully we can meet again?" she said, with questioning eyes.

"Maybe," said Riley, turning on her heel and walking away before her mother could see the tears rolling down her cheeks.

Riley went straight home to Sundance. Lost in her own thoughts, she went about the routine of catching him from his field, grooming him and tacking him up. "Come on boy, let's go running."

Riley guided Sundance down the drive and along the country lanes until they reached the track that would take them to the open moors. She carefully manoeuvred Sundance as she opened, then closed the gate behind her. She breathed in deeply, inhaling the fresh, autumnal air, and asked Sundance to trot. Sundance, ears pricked, trotting briskly, eagerly awaiting Riley's cue to increase his pace. And there it was, a gentle squeeze and they were gone. His canter swiftly pushed into a gallop from Riley's cue, his powerful legs covering the undulating moorland ground confidently at high speed, and with the feeling of his thundering hooves beneath her, she let go. Galloping hard and fast, the biting wind whipping around her, tears streamed down her face. The hurt, the anger, the constant disappointment, the fear, all bubbling up and pouring out of her as she and Sundance galloped as one.

Jem

Jem looked down at her beautiful Tilly, now eight weeks old, and reluctantly handed her over to Ben.

"I promise you, you will feel better for it. Trust me Jem," said Ben with pleading eyes.

Jem knew Ben was struggling to understand her constantly depressed mood. He didn't know what to do, or how to help her. He did as much as he could for her during his nine weeks paternity leave from work, but on Monday morning, he would be back to work and she would be left alone with Tilly, and the majority of house chores, and Pandora. Ben took over all duties relating to Pandora as soon as Tilly was born, insisting that Jem needed rest. She needed time to bond with Tilly, and to help Noah bond with Tilly too. And of course, she shouldn't be carrying heavy buckets and bales of hay around after just having a baby. Overwhelmed with a newborn, and the cloud of misery that had engulfed her since the birth, Jem agreed. And now Jem was nervous of going back to the yard. She was worried about having to see her friends and pretend she was ok, but Ben was adamant. And no matter how awful she felt, she would not neglect her horse.

Jem felt emotion swell inside as she watched her horse eagerly trot towards her when she went to catch her from the paddock. She stretched out her hand for her mare to sniff and was greeted with Pandora's deep nicker. The sound itself made Jem realise how much she missed her friend, and she enveloped her in a warm embrace, burying her head in her mane and breathing in her delicious horsey smell. She put Pandora's headcollar on, then gently tugged the lead rope and Pandora followed her down to the yard.

Jem focused only on her horse. Her usual busy, negative brain calmed, and she quickly fell into the daily care routine for Pandora. Rhythmically grooming her body, she slowly began to tell Pandora her secrets. "I feel so alone, I feel so ashamed for being such a bad mum. I feel I don't give enough attention to Noah because I'm so busy with Tilly. I feel I'm not giving Tilly enough attention because I'm so worried about Noah. I feel I'm neglecting Ben. I can't remember the last time I cooked him a decent meal or washed the football kits. I'm failing in every which way I turn. Help me, Pandora, please help me. I don't know what to do."

Pandora turned to face Jem, and gently rested her head on her shoulder, emitting another of her soft, deep, intimate nickers.

Jem closed her eyes and lent her head against Pandora, her arms circling around her mare, silent, just being with her horse. The tears flowed, but no sound came. Jem cried silent, private tears, with the only friend she knew wouldn't judge her, the only friend she could trust.

When finally there were no more tears to shed, Pandora carefully lifted her head and looked at Jem with her kind, gentle, liquid brown eyes, and blinked.

"My darling Pandora, my dearest friend, I'm sorry I've been away for you so long," Jem said, looking into the eyes of her forgiving friend. She kissed Pandora on her nose, untied the lead rope, and together, they slowly walked back to the paddock.

"Thank you for listening to me. I'll see you tomorrow," Jem told the little mare, before turning away and walking back to the car, feeling ever so slightly lighter than on arrival.

Rose

Rose was sitting in front her computer, a glass of wine in hand and her fluffy ginger cat snoozing next to her on the desk. She looked at the screen and said aloud, with a determined voice, "It's time to be proactive." Then she typed the words *mini break destinations in Devon* into her computer search engine. "See," she said to her sleeping cat. "I'm going to take a break."

Rose had been true to her word and contacted the town vet. Her friend, and former colleague, Sarah, was thrilled to receive her call, explaining they had just taken on a new vet, and were able to take on any extra work she might have. Providing cover for next weekend and working with her and some of her clients would not be a problem at all.

Rose felt like a weight had been lifted after hanging up the phone to Sarah. *Now I need time for myself, time to rest and recharge,* she thought, determined to make herself take a step back from work and focus on getting better. *What use will I be if I burn myself out? That's a recipe for disaster. I could make a silly mistake, a silly fatal mistake,* she firmly told herself. *It is in my clients' best interests for me to get myself back on top form.*

Scrolling through the adverts online, she came across a small hotel in south Devon, and judging by the photographs, it looked to be situated in an idyllic spot near the seaside. "Yes," she said out loud. "Bracing long walks on the beach, the sea air will do me the world of good. And they have a small spa offering relaxing massages," she told her cat. "I think this is the one."

She poured herself another glass of wine for Dutch courage and took a generous swig, then entered her details into the computer and booked herself three nights away. Her first break away in a very long time. Longer than she could even remember.

Rose left for work with a spring her step the following morning. A bleak early November morning filled with mist and drizzle did not dampen her mood. Excitement starting to fizz inside her for her mini holiday.

"Hello Ellen, hi David," she called out when she arrived at the address Ellen had sent her two days ago. She'd asked her to come and take a look at another potential horse.

Ellen smiled warmly at her "Hi Rose, thanks for coming. You seem chirpy!"

"I am," Rose replied. "I've been as good as my word - I booked my break away last night."

"What great news! Oh, look here he comes now," said Ellen, pointing to a gorgeous horse being led out of his stable. "I actually know the owner; she's one of my clients. Unfortunately, she's struggling to manage her three horses now as she's just had her fourth child. She called me yesterday for advice and when she found out I was looking for a horse, she offered me first refusal of her 15 hand, jet black, pure Andalusian - beautiful isn't he? His name is Jupiter."

"Indeed, he is, and he looks in excellent condition. Hopefully coming from a trusted source, we won't have the same problem as last time," Rose said ruefully.

She watched carefully when the owner trotted Jupiter up the yard, then she began her physical examination of him.

David, Rose and Jupiter's owner stood back and watched Ellen work Jupiter in the sand school. His poise and elegance, coupled with Ellen's skill, gave the onlookers a treat as they performed exercises that resembled a regal dance.

"Doesn't she look wonderful," Rose said,

"I think she's found the one. I haven't seen her ride like that with any other horse except Sundance," David replied, his eyes not leaving the mesmerizing duo.

Ellen and Jupiter trotted over. "He is amazing!" gushed Ellen, patting the horse's neck in praise with a radiating glow surrounding her and Jupiter.

"Well, he looks in fantastic condition from what I've seen today, but I'm afraid I can't give you my professional opinion until I get the samples back from the lab. I'll send them off today so hopefully you won't have to wait too long," Rose explained to Ellen.

Leaving the yard, Rose headed off to her next client, praying that the test results would bring good news for Ellen.

Riley

Riley and Joe talked long into the night about her mother. Riley believed that her mother had changed and begun to turn her life around, but she was struggling to forgive her. Joe assured her that it would take time, and she must go at her own pace. Nell would just have to accept that.

The question was, what to do about Molly? She was so young, only six when Riley took her away. She didn't remember the extent of her mother's toxic behaviour because Riley had always shielded her from it the best she could. Was it fair of Riley to deny Molly her mother? Just because she wasn't ready to forgive and move on, that didn't mean Molly felt the same.

After many hours, sitting in front of the cosy log burner, drinking cups of tea, Joe helped her to reach a decision. Molly was eight now, old enough to have an opinion that Riley should take into consideration. Joe reassured her that since she was Molly's legal guardian now, her mother couldn't take her away from her, nor did she have to let Molly see her. The final decision was Riley's to make, but it was only fair to ask Molly what she would like to do.

They decided that this was a conversation that should take place just between Riley and Molly, and in a neutral setting, out riding.

Riley woke the following morning feeling lighter after having discussed her worries and fears with Joe. It felt like they now had a plan to help them move forward with the situation. Sitting around the breakfast table, the sisters munching scrambled eggs and toast, Riley announced that she was taking Molly riding, and if she got all of her chores for Pipsqueak sorted before they left, she'd let them loose on the canter track.

Molly jumped up. "Yay!" she said to her sister, "I'll get started right now, I promise I'll get everything done." Taking her toast with her, she scampered off to the yard.

Riley smiled as she tidied up the kitchen after the breakfast onslaught. Molly was so happy here. Clare and Joe were now very much a part of her family, and she was so grateful for the calm and friendly home life they helped her provide for Molly.

A little while later, they were nearly at the canter track. "Are you ready?" Riley asked the eager little girl trotting along behind her.

"Yes, Riley, we're ready," Molly replied.

"Now mind you keep that little monster of yours behind Sundance at all times, you got it?"

"I will, I promise Pipsqueak will behave. Can we go now?"

During their time in Australia, Molly had spent many hours playing ponies with the daughter of the owner of the stables where Joe and Riley were working. She'd been fully immersed in the day-to-day life of horses, and now that she lived at Hollybrook stables, she was becoming a proficient rider. She doted on Pipsqueak, tying pink ribbons in his mane and tail and painting his hooves in sparkly hoof oil, and she never regaled on her responsibilities for looking after him. Riley very much enjoyed taking her out riding now that she could ride competently on her own and she was learning to control her little mischief maker in canter out hacking.

"Ok, let's go," Riley called out, squeezing Sundance into a nice steady canter. Sundance always knew when he was babysitting Molly and had perfected his pace for the little pony scooting up behind him. Not too fast, and not too slow.

"Come on, Pipsqueak," Riley heard Molly say to her pony, then there was a series of squeaks and squeals as the little girl and her pony smoothly transitioned to canter, keeping up with Sundance.

Riley turned to check on her. *Phew,* she thought. *Still where she should be, sitting on top of her pony!*

"Keep going, Riley, don't stop!" Molly called out, with Pipsqueak's little legs cantering along at ten to the dozen.

Riley and Sundance continued their steady canter, to the whoops of delight from Molly behind, until they neared the end of the track.

"That's it, Molls, no more track, bring him down to trot," Riley instructed her.

Grinning from ear to ear, Molly slowed her pony then brought Pipsqueak alongside Sundance, and they plodded home along the lanes.

"Thanks Riley," Molly said, with a beaming smile.

"Molls, I need to talk to you about something. It's about Mum."

"Ok," said Molly, stretching down to pat Pipsqueak on his neck.

"I saw her last week. She's getting better. She's not like she used to be. Would you like to see her?"

"Will you be there?" Molly asked.

"Yes, of course," replied Riley.

"Will I come back home to Hollybrook? I don't want her to take me away!"

"Yes, you live at Hollybrook Molly, and you will always live with me. I just wanted to let you know that you could see her if you wanted too?"

"Ok then, if you'll be with me, we can see her."

Riley felt secretly pleased that her relationship with Molly was as strong as she hoped it was, and that her sister wanted to be with her. Chose to be with her. Feeling like the ride went well, she felt the whirling in her mind, that had been there since she saw her mother last week, finally beginning to settle. They plodded home, side by side, and Riley listened quietly as Molly chatted away about her beloved Pipsqueak and the new friend she made at school.

Rose

Rose slid between the pristine white Egyptian sheets and sighed with contentment. *This holiday malarkey is starting to grow on me,* she thought, stretching out like a starfish on the queen-sized bed. In the tranquillity of her hotel room, Rose reflected on her perfect day.

Before leaving her little cottage early in the morning, Rose couldn't help herself - she had to check her emails, just in case. Logging on to her computer, she vowed to herself that this would be the only work act she would commit until nine o clock on Monday morning. The email sitting in her inbox removed any traces of guilt that she felt when she opened up the report from the lab regarding Ellen's potential horse. All blood tests were clear. *What a relief,* Rose thought, smiling at the computer for delivering her such good news for the start of her holiday.

Rose pinged off a quick message to Ellen:

Professional opinion...Buy Jupiter!!

All tests clear x

A reply beeped through instantly:

Fantastic news, thank you.

Stop working!

Enjoy your holiday x

Rose buckled up and started her car, excitement simmering inside about the mini adventure ahead of her. She turned the car radio up and sang her heart out as she made her way to the picturesque Devonshire coast.

The hotel delivered everything they advertised on the website, and then some. Warmly greeted by the receptionist, Rose was quickly settled into her hotel suite with the offer of any help she might need during her stay. Rose looked out of her Georgian window and watched the waves crashing on the beach. Although grey and misty early winter weather, it was dry. Changing into her walking boots and heavy coat, she set off to explore and enjoy a walk along the sand. The biting wind brought colour to her drawn, pale skin, and the exertion reignited her adrenaline as she briskly strode across the barren beach.

A massage in the relaxing spa followed, and the kind receptionist generously offered to bring her supper up to her room on a tray so she could enjoy a long soak in the complimentary aromatherapy bubble bath oils the hotel provided and continue her day of pampering.

Snuggled down between the Egyptian sheets and deep maroon coloured duvet cover, listening to the wind howling and rain hammering on her window, she switched off the light and closed her eyes.

RING...RING, boomed the hotel phone, sitting on the bedside table right next to her ear.

RING...RING, it went again.

"You have got to be kidding me," Rose said out loud, flicking the light on and picking up the receiver.

"Hello?" she said.

"Hello, is that Rose?" a voice that she didn't recognise crackled down the line.

"Yes, speaking."

"You're a vet?" The curt question was asked in a hurried tone.

"Yes, I'm a vet. Who are you? How did you get this number?" Rose asked, annoyed at having her peaceful night interrupted by a stranger.

"I'm so terribly sorry to bother you but it's an emergency. The local vet has been called out on another job and won't be back for hours and I feel that it will be too late by then. Can you help?"

"I'm on my way," Rose answered. *Even in a secluded holiday spot a vet's life is never her own,* she thought, throwing off the duvet covers and dressing quickly. Rose's caring disposition meant she was never able to turn an animal in need down, and curiosity was niggling at her as to who the stranger was at the end of the phone. How did she know she was a vet? And what on earth was this emergency?

Andrew

Andrew waited patiently in the hotel lobby for the vet he had just disturbed to arrive. A fleeting thought that he might have ruined her holiday was soon outweighed by the gravity of the situation and the necessity for a qualified vet to act as quickly as possible in such a tragic case. *That must be her,* he thought, watching a petite woman bundled up in heavy outdoor wear hurry over to the reception desk.

"Andrew," his sister, the receptionist, called out to him and waved him over. "This is Rose, the vet I told you about."

Holding out his hand in greeting, which Rose accepted and firmly shook, he explained, "I'm Andrew, the local animal welfare officer. I received a call this evening about a horse, and I'm going to prepare you, it is one of the most tragic animal cases I have ever seen."

The woman looked at him gravely as she listened. "I'm not a vet so I can't make the call, but I think the poor creature needs to be put out of its misery as soon as possible."

"We had better get going then," Rose said with a blank expression on her face.

Holding the door open, he watched her brace herself against the torrential rain, and run to her car to collect her vet case, then return to him. Together they dashed to his car, finally escaping the rain.

"She's about twenty minutes away," Andrew told her, feeling guilty about what he was about to expose this woman too.

"A mare?" Rose asked.

"Yes, roughly 16 hands I would say, although hard to tell with just a torch and the state she's in."

Rose quietly nodded.

"So, I'm guessing your sister, the receptionist, told you I was a vet?"

"Yes, I rang her in desperation to find out if she knew of anyone that could help, and as luck would have it, you checked into the hotel today."

They continued the rest of the journey in silence. *No doubt she is mentally preparing herself for what she will be walking into,* he thought. *Just like I am, and I already know.* Anger surged through him that animals could be treated in such a barbaric way.

Turning down the pothole-filled dirt track and pointing to a half fallen-down shack, he told Rose, "This is it, we're here."

Rose silently got out of the car and followed him. The wind was stinging his cheeks and relentless rain was pounding against them as they sloshed their way through the thick, heavy mud. The stench hit them as soon as they stepped into the shack. Keeping the torch beam on the floor he waited for Rose to catch her breath. "Are you ready?" he asked, and he saw her nod her head.

Slowly raising the beam of light, amidst the dank, gloomy shelter and stinking filth, they saw her. He heard Rose gasp as she took in the frightful creature before their eyes. Nothing more than a skeleton with rough patches of fur amidst the pus-filled, weeping wounds all over her body.

"It's ok, girl," he heard Rose murmur, as she slowly made her way towards the frightened horse. "I'm not going to hurt you."

The quietly composed woman set her case down on the muck-ridden floor and slowly pulled out her stethoscope. She reached out her hand for the horse to sniff, then slowly placed the stethoscope against her and listened to her heartbeat.

Andrew stood quietly and watched her work, secretly impressed at how she was managing to keep herself together and behave in such a professional manner. He was pleased that he had been lucky enough to find someone who was more than capable to do the job that he felt would need to be done.

Rose took out her chip reader and gently scanned her neck, bringing a surprise to both of them when it beeped, acknowledging a chip. "Her name is Winter's Rescue, she's twelve years old and has a registered address," she told Andrew.

Andrew immediately felt motivated to pursue the evil owners who had done this to their horse and hoped that justice would be served. He would be searching them down as soon as dawn broke and alerting the authorities to the cruelty.

"Is it time now?" he asked Rose.

"Time for what?" she replied, with a quizzical look in her eyes.

"To put the poor thing out of her misery," he said in a grave voice.

"I'm not putting her down," remarked Rose to his surprise. "I'm going to take her to Hollybrook stables and get her better." Taking her phone out of her pocket, she continued. "I'm going to make arrangements for her transport. She's not staying here any longer than she has to."

Suzie

Suzie and her family arrived home glowing with golden tans and full of wonderful stories about the amazing family honeymoon they had experienced. It really was the holiday of a lifetime and everything they had hoped and wished it would be. But of course it didn't take long for them to fall back into the routine life of work, school and horses.

Suzie was settled at home, ironing school uniforms, with the boys fast asleep. She was chatting to Luke about Clarissa, and asking if he would help them with some jumping tomorrow. Then her phone rang.

"Blimey," she said to Luke, looking at her watch. "Who could that be at this hour?"

Seeing Ellen's name flash up on the screen she clicked to accept the call.

"Suze, great to have you home, emergency, I need you, can you come with me to Devon to pick up a rescue horse and Rose please?"

"Right now?" Suzie asked, hoping she was mistaking Ellen's tone and she meant first thing in the morning.

"Yep, right now. Is Luke home to watch the boys?"

"Yes, he is. When will you be here?"

"I'm outside, come on, get a wiggle on, no time to waste," said Ellen.

"Emergency, something to do with Rose and a horse, I have to go!" Suzie told Luke as she placed a kiss on the top of his head.

Her husband knew full well that she could never turn down an animal or friend in need, and she was grateful for his instant, supportive reply.

"Keep me updated and let me know when you arrive, and stay safe," said Luke, pulling his wife towards him to return her kiss.

Wellington boots and rain jacket on, Suzie said, "Will do!" and gave him a quick wave, before heading out into the pouring rain to meet Ellen.

"What's the news?" she asked Ellen as soon as she climbed into the warm cab of the horse lorry.

"Limited intel I'm afraid. Sick horse, needs emergency transport to Hollybrook." She shoved a crumpled piece of paper into Suzie's hands. "Here, I wrote the address down."

The first twenty minutes of the journey were spent deliberating over what was actually going on with Rose, but as neither of them knew the full story, nor would they until they arrived, their conversation turned towards life at Hollybrook and their friends.

"How's Jem?" Suzie enquired. "I hardly heard from her when I was away, even though I sent her loads of pictures and the boys sent videos for Noah."

Ellen seemed to mull the question over. "Actually, come to think of it, I've hardly seen her myself."

"But you're always at the yard!" Suzie exclaimed. "How can you not have seen her?"

"Well, I've seen Ben quite a bit, but not much of Jem," Ellen replied.

That seems strange, Suzie thought. *Jem was always at the yard - any free time she had would be spent with Pandora. Maybe she's busy with Tilly,* she mused. *But just in case something is up, I'll pop over and see her soon.*

"Are you sure this is it?" Ellen queried. "I think it will be a struggle to get this horsebox down that dirt track."

"Definitely, I saw the name on the sign that you have written down on this piece of paper, we must have driven the two miles by now. Why don't we park up and I'll walk down?" said Suzie, apprehension starting to rise in her at the thought of walking down a dirt track, into the unknown, in the middle of a storm. Then she added, "Maybe we should walk together?"

"Agreed," said Ellen, zipping up her coat and pulling on her woolly hat.

Woefully unprepared in their haste, they only had their mobile phones to use as torches. Linking arms to help keep each other up in the wet, slippery mud, they marched down the eerie track.

Seeing the car Rose described over the phone, Ellen shouted to be heard over the howling wind. "This is the place!" Together they headed over to the rambling shack.

They were met by a tall man, blocking the entrance. He stepped aside to let them in.

"Prepare yourselves, ladies. It isn't a pretty sight," he said, then flipped his torch beam into the corner for them to see Rose and Winter.

"Oh, holy Jesus above," Ellen exclaimed, not moving a muscle.

"Bloody hell," gasped Suzie.

"Hi guys," said Rose, leaving the mare's side and putting her arms around her friends. "Thank you so much for coming. I've given her something for the pain, but we need to get her out of here right now."

"Damn right we do," said Ellen.

"This is Andrew," Rose said, gesturing to Andrew. "He's the animal welfare officer that called me."

After briefly introducing themselves, Suzie and Ellen left the shack to get the horse box. There was no way that horse could walk up the track. They would have to bring the box to her.

Settled back in the cab of the horse box, Ellen navigated the treacherous road. "I've never seen anything like it," Suzie quietly told Ellen.

"Nor have I, I felt physically sick when I saw her," Ellen confided.

"Me too," replied Suzie. "I'm so pleased you called me, the more hands the better for this situation. And Rose is going to need all the help she can get once we get the mare back to Hollybrook."

Pulling up as close to the ramshackle shack as possible, Suzie and Ellen braced themselves against the relentless storm for the second time and lifted down the tail board.

"Ok, we're ready, try and see if you can load her," called out Ellen.

Suzie watched Rose tug on the makeshift halter that she had placed on the mare. Suzie never failed to be impressed by her friend's calm capability with animals. She noticed Rose give a gentle tug on the rope and the trusting mare followed her out of the filthy hovel and into the horse lorry, emitting a large sigh when Rose undid the halter and placed a small slice of hay in front of her.

She heard Rose quietly soothing the mare, "everything is going to be ok now, girl. I'm going to look after you." Then she gave the horse a gentle stroke on her nose, before sliding out of the jockey door and signalling for Suzie to close up the tail board.

"I'll call you as soon as I get her settled at Hollybrook," Rose called out to Andrew, as the three of them piled into the cab.

Ellen started up the engine and Suzie put her arms around Rose.

"What a day," Suzie said. "Now let's go home."

Jem

"But you said you felt a little bit better after seeing Pandora," Ben said, with an edge of frustration in his voice.

"I just don't feel up to going to the yard today," Jem explained to Ben. And she didn't. She didn't feel much like doing anything. Ten weeks since Tilly arrived and the relentless mist of misery that had seemed to swallow her up was still ever present.

"Jem, I think you need to speak to someone," Ben said. "I don't know why you're so unhappy all the time, I just don't know how to help you. Please, will you speak to one of your friends? You never know, it might just help. Or maybe we should go and ask a doctor for advice? I just don't know what to do."

Ben looked at her with pleading eyes, and she knew he was being patient with her, and he was trying, but she didn't know herself why her moods swung from tears, to anxiety, to complete lack of self-worth. And deep down, she knew she couldn't carry on like this, so reluctantly she agreed to message Suzie and ask if she wanted to go riding.

Ben kept staring at her.

"Ok, I'll message her now," she relented.

Suzie's reply came through instantly, saying she would meet her on the yard in half an hour. Jem showed the message to Ben.

Tentatively smiling at her, he said, "I'll drop you off."

Ben gave her hand a gentle, affectionate squeeze when she opened the car door. "Try and have fun with your friend," he said, as she climbed out of the car, feeling like a black cloud was hanging over her.

"Hi Jem," Suzie called out, leading both Clarissa and Pandora onto the yard.

Jem felt there was nothing else for her to do but slap her smile on her face and get through the next hour as best she could.

"Hi Suze, how was your holiday?" she asked.

And that was it. Suzie chatted nonstop, going into great detail about her fantastic holiday, and Jem quietly went about the business of getting Pandora ready, barely taking a word in that Suzie was saying.

Jem silently climbed into Pandora's saddle, and with the idea to keep Suzie talking, said, "Tell me more about the elephants." And Suzie continued to waffle on about the elephants bathing in the water as they plodded down the lane.

Jem felt Suzie's eyes on her. "Are you ok, Jem?" she asked. "You've barely said a word."

"Just tired, you know what it's like with a newborn," replied Jem, hoping that would satisfy her. It didn't.

"I hope you don't mind me saying but, well you don't seem like your usual self. Are you sure you're feeling ok?" Suzie asked, looking at her with kind, thoughtful eyes.

Jem felt a lump form in her throat. The pressure of trying to keep herself together was becoming too much, then slowly, a tear crept out of the corner of her eye and trickled down her cheek.

"Oh Jem," Suzie cried, pulling Clarissa to a halt, jumping out of the saddle and walking over to her friend. "What is it? What's the matter?"

And there, in the middle of a country lane, sitting on her horse, Jem broke down and told Suzie how she really felt. Suzie stood next to her, listening intently whilst she explained her feelings of hopelessness and the perpetual black cloud that she felt engulfing her.

"I know how you feel Jem, I felt exactly like that after I had Joseph. I think you're suffering with post-natal depression. It's actually surprisingly common, but for some reason it seems to be a taboo topic. I felt like I was walking through sludge every single day for months. I felt all the same feelings of life overwhelming me and hopelessness, and then one day, poof, it vanished. I woke up one morning and felt like the cloud had lifted, as seems to be the way with these things."

Jem listened to Suzie in amazement. "You felt just like I'm feeling now?" she enquired.

"Yes, exactly the same. I promise you; you'll start to feel better soon and the best thing you can do is be with your family and friends and lean on them. Accept their support until you start to feel better. And Pandora, of course! Spend as much time with Pandora as you can. Every time I left Clarissa, I felt a teeny-weeny bit better, and over time, all the little bits started to add up and I started to feel better for longer periods of time. Never doubt the healing power of horses," Suzie told her seriously.

Jem looked down at her kind and caring friend. She felt ever so slightly lighter, now that she knew there was a small glimmer of light at the end of the dark, gloomy tunnel she was temporarily encased in.

"Now," said Suzie. "Should I get back on Clarissa and we continue our ride?"

Smiling down at her friend, Jem replied, "Yes, let's go riding. Thank you, Suzie."

Rose

Rose couldn't explain it, but somehow, she just knew she needed to save the horse. The first time she reached out to her and felt the mare's whiskers graze over her hand, she felt a connection with her. A kind of deep-rooted, raw, animalistic desire to save her. A feeling that she and the mare were meant to be together. That the reason for her mini break wasn't to rest at all. It was to be in that hotel, at that time, so she could be the first vet to see Winter. To know that the broken-down mare should not be put to sleep but nurtured and loved. This animal was not ready to cross that rainbow bridge. And she didn't know why she knew, but she just did, even though the mare was in the most pitiful, tragic state she had ever witnessed a horse to be in.

Easing up on her practice work now seemed to be a blessing in disguise, allowing her time she would not otherwise have had, to dedicate herself to Winter's recovery. She also spent a few very profitable hours surfing the internet trying find any information available about the mare, and she was in luck. Winter appeared to be an ex-racehorse. Winter's Rescue, many years ago, in her prime, was a first-class winning racehorse. The pictures she found of her showed a powerful, beautiful, bright bay thoroughbred. A far cry from the weeping, wound-filled, skeletal creature that Rose had discovered her to be. *How on earth did she go from winning racehorse to abused neglected skeleton?* Rose wondered. *I guess I will never know. It will always be one of the great mysteries of life, and Winter will never be able to tell me.*

Winter had been at the yard for two weeks, and what a difference two weeks of food, kindness and veterinary treatment had made. Her eyes were brighter, the wounds were healing well, and a little spark seemed to have ignited within her, as if she knew she was being helped and she would do all she could to help get herself better.

Everyone on the yard loved her, once they got over the shock of her current outward appearance. Her kind and gentle temperament shone through, and anyone passing her stable or paddock was greeted with a soft whinny.

The morning after she took Winter from the stinking hovel, she messaged Andrew asking what the protocol was for the paperwork side of things, in order for her to keep Winter. For Winter to be her own horse. Andrew was thrilled at the idea, explaining that the charity stables he worked alongside were always overflowing with unwanted, neglected and abused horses. If Rose wanted to keep her, it would free up a space for another horse in need and he would get the paperwork sorted straight away. He would come and visit Winter soon. He explained that it would be something of a tick box exercise, to ensure that she was in a suitable environment and well cared for, to then enable him to sign her over to Rose.

Rose felt excitement fizzle through her with the knowledge that Winter would be hers. Never again would the mare be subjected to any kind of cruelty. Rose would keep her safe.

Rose let herself into Winter's stable. It was time for her evening feed and for the medicated ointment to be applied to her wounds. Winter nickered at Rose when she saw her.

"Dinner time," Rose exclaimed, placing her feed bowl on the floor for her. Rose liked being at the stables at night. It was calm and quiet and brought her a sense of peace that she hadn't felt in a very long time.

Riley

"Come on, Molly. It's time to go," Riley shouted up the stairs to her sister. Today was the day, the day Molly would see their mum. Riley hadn't slept a wink last night. Her mind whizzing round with what ifs. What if she let them down? What if she tried to take Molly away? What if she upset Molly? But she knew she couldn't back out now. Once the date had been set, Molly had become excited about the impending visit.

Riley had chosen a neutral meeting place, a small café in town, allowing enough time for a quick drink and an easy get away if needed, as well as the option to order some food and take their time if she felt that things were going well.

Nell was waiting for them when they walked in, and Molly went racing to her and straight in for a hug. Riley, far more reserved and cautious, offered, "Hi Mum," before taking a seat on the opposite side of the table.

The conversation was somewhat stagnated, Molly quiet in her seat, picking up on the tension between her sister and mother. When the waitress left with their order, breaking the awkward silence, her mother produced a bag and said, "I have something for you, Molly. Riley tells me you are just as horse mad as she is, you even have your own pony." She handed over a pony colouring book, colouring pencil pack and sheet of sparkly pony stickers.

"Ohhhh, for me?" said Molly, accepting the gift. "I love ponies, mine is called Pipsqueak!" Then she promptly set about colouring in her new book.

Nell then looked at Riley. "I have something for you, too," she said, then handed her a small box.

Riley opened the box to find her grandmother's pearl necklace inside, a gift her grandmother had given to her mother just before she passed away. Riley remembered playing with the necklace as a child. It was one of the few happy memories she had involving her mother, when they played dress up together and Riley was allowed to wear her mother's most precious item, the pearl necklace.

"Grandma's necklace," she said, taking it out of the box and running it through her fingers.

"I know how much you always loved it, I thought you might like it. Something pretty to wear for a special occasion," Nell replied.

Riley was speechless. She had no idea that her mother even knew how special the necklace was to her. She was pleasantly surprised to realise her mother could be so thoughtful.

The little trio, settled in the warm café on a wintery grey day, chatted companionably for two hours.

"It's time to go now, Molly. We have to give the horses their evening feed," she told her sister.

"Can Mum come?" Molly asked. "I'd like her to meet Pipsqueak."

Riley felt panic building inside her. They had all enjoyed a pleasant afternoon, but she was in no way ready for her mother to step into their world at Hollybrook stables.

Her mother must have picked up on her distress, because she turned to Molly and said, "I would love to come and meet Pipsqueak, but I'm afraid I can't come today. Riley and I will organise a date soon though, ok?"

"Ok," Molly replied, her attention focused on packing away her colouring book and pencils. "Come on, Riley. I don't want to keep Pipsqueak waiting."

Riley gave her mother a smile in gratitude. "Yes, we'll plan another date soon. Come along, Molls. We can't keep your pony waiting."

Andrew

Andrew turned into Hollybrook stables drive and pulled up in the car park. The first thing he saw was a lady riding a beautiful jet-black horse. They were flying over ginormous jumps in the sand school. And then he saw Rose waving to him from the yard. She looked different to how he remembered her. *But then, she was bundled up into so many layers it was difficult to know what she looked like,* he thought.

He climbed out of his car and strolled over to meet her. He was met with a warm friendly smile and beautiful hazel eyes. *Very pretty, how did I not notice that before?* he thought, looking down at the petite lady with brown hair curling around her neck, underneath the purple woolly hat she was wearing.

"Hi Rose," he said.

"Hi Andrew, come and see Winter, she's in the stable just over here."

"Oh my word. Wow! She looks like a completely different horse!" he exclaimed, when Winter popped her head over the stable door in friendly greeting.

"She's improved so much, hasn't she?" Rose said, proudly looking up at Winter. "Of course, we still have a very long way to go, but she's improving every day. We even went for a little walk-in hand yesterday. She loved being out and about, exploring her new surroundings."

Andrew couldn't believe the improvement in Winter, not only physically but in herself, too. Clear, bright eyes looked kindly at him, then a nose inquisitively snuffled him. She was so friendly. After what the horse had suffered from human hands, he was baffled that she could be so forgiving. And the credit lay with Rose. He could feel it when they were together. He felt it in the filthy shack when they first met, and he could feel it now. Winter and Rose had an unexplainable bond, a bond that was formed the instant they met.

Rose had this air about her, a kind, calm aura whenever she was around animals. They seemed to know she spoke their language and that they could trust her. And Andrew was beginning to feel that he also, very much liked to be in her company.

During the car journey to Hollybrook he had decided that it would be best to give Rose the bad news first. He knew she would be disappointed but unfortunately there was nothing he was able do about it. He had exhausted all options available to him.

With a grave voice he announced, "I have some bad news I'm afraid, Rose." He noticed her face fall and swiftly continued. He wanted to get this over and done with as quickly as possible. "I have searched high and low for Winter's owners in order to bring them to justice for what they did to her. Unfortunately, the microchip details are out of date, and the information I've been able to retrieve doesn't give us any answers. The gist of it is, the owner registered on the chip has passed away, and left behind a lot of debt. A family member sold off, gave away or part exchanged... well we don't really know, but they disposed of all of the horses, and we have no paper trail at all. We have no idea how Winter ended up where she did. I'm so very sorry that no one will be held accountable for what has happened to her."

He watched Rose and waited quietly for her to process the information he had just given her.

Eventually, she was ready to reply. "But she's safe now, and that's all that really matters, isn't it?"

"Yes," he responded, nodding in agreement, silently impressed again by this pragmatic, capable and compassionate woman.

"I also have good news," he announced, reaching into his pocket and handing over what he knew Rose was waiting for, the paperwork that stated that Winter now belonged to her. He watched her unfold the paper, skim read down, and then she saw it. A large smile spread across her face, giving it away.

"There it is, in black and white," she said to him, pointing at the paper, "I'm Winter's owner."

He smiled down at her and laughed, "I know," he said. "I'm the one that wrote it!"

Suzie

Suzie arrived on the yard, bursting with excitement to see Ellen ride her new horse Jupiter. She had met him when he arrived a few days ago, but weekday work and family duties prevented her from giving him anything more than a swift stroke with the promise of getting to know him properly soon.

"Wowsers, he's a beaut," she said to Ellen, climbing out of her car and walking over to the sand school.

"I know," Ellen agreed, trotting the elegant horse over to her. "And did you see him clear the four-foot spread?"

"I did, I watched as I drove up the drive. He cleared it like a champ," Suzie said, offering the much-deserved praise to the gorgeous horse standing before her.

"Hang on a minute, who's that talking to Rose?" Suzie said, nodding in the direction of Rose and the strange man.

"Don't you recognise him?" Ellen laughed. "That's Andrew, the animal welfare guy."

"Really? I'll just pop over and say hello," Suzie announced. "Don't do anything exciting with Jupiter until I get back!" she called out over her shoulder.

"Hi Rose, hi Andrew," Suzie said. "Remember me? I was one of the rescue transport crew," she laughed, as she re-introduced herself.

"Of course, how could I forget," he replied. "Hasn't Rose done a wonderful job with Winter?"

"Oh yes, she's like a different horse. Rose has a magical ability to cure horses," Suzie said, smiling proudly at her friend.

"I only wish that we could find more people like Rose to take ownership of some of the other rescued horses we have in our overspilling rescue centres."

"How many more?" Suzie enquired, intrigued to learn more about his interesting job.

"Hundreds, literally hundreds, Suzie. Our shelters are permanently filled to the brim. And as soon as a space becomes available, we have ten plus more in need to take its place."

Suzie was shocked and horrified at the magnitude of the ongoing problem people like Andrew were trying to tackle every day, with limited resources, lack of funding and staff shortages.

"And are the general public allowed to visit these rescue centres? See for themselves the work you guys do and all the animals in need of a home?"

"Yes, of course. We open the centres to raise money. The public who visit often leave donations for us to help us to continue what we do," Andrew explained.

"I'd like to visit one please," Suzie announced, unable to explain the mixed emotions she was beginning to feel. *How can there be so many unwanted horses? I need to see this for myself,* she thought.

"No problem, I'll give you the details. You can either come during opening hours, or if you like, you could come after closing and I could take you on a little tour of the centre, explain everything to you, introduce you to some of the residents?" Andrew said, then turned to look at Rose. "You too, Rose."

"Yes please, we would love a private tour, wouldn't we Rose?" Suzie said, giving Rose a sly wink. Andrew extending the invitation to Rose, and the way he had looked at her, had not gone unnoticed by Suzie.

Suzie noticed Rose blush before replying, "Ok, I'm in. Could I bring a friend along as well please?"

"Oh, me too, can I bring a friend as well?" Suzie asked, thinking Jem could really do with a trip out. They could all get supper together on the way home.

Laughing, Andrew replied, "of course, the more the merrier!"

Jem

Jem received a message from Suzie:

The gang's going on a road trip.

Horses and food.

I'll pick you up tomorrow x

"What is she up too now?" Jem chuckled, passing her phone to Ben to read the message for himself.

"Who knows?" Ben laughed in reply. "But I guess you'll find out when she picks you up tomorrow."

Ben looked at Jem, and she knew he could tell she was having doubts about going. She was just managing to get her daily routine under control, and the thought of going somewhere unknown was beginning to bring on feelings of anxiety.

"I think you should go, Jem. All the girls are going. It will only be for a few hours, you'll have fun."

"Ok," she sighed. "I'll go."

The next morning, Jem woke with the usual cloud of gloom around her and forced herself up. As the days passed, she was slowly but surely finding little bits of enjoyment in life, but she had to push past the morning haze first. She heard Tilly crying and scooped her up to pacify her.

"Mum, is breakfast ready?" Noah called out from his bedroom. Her day had begun.

Wandering downstairs to prepare everyone's breakfast, she was met with a freshly laid breakfast table, with a parcel sitting on her plate.

"For me?" she asked Ben.

"Yes, for you," he said, coming over to her to give her a morning kiss. "I thought you could wear it out for dinner with the girls. It's only casual, I know you're doing horsey stuff first, but still, I thought you deserved a treat."

Jem felt a glimmer of happiness penetrating through the gloom, at the actions of her thoughtful partner. She was still carrying some baby weight and complained to Ben that none of her clothes fitted properly, and she felt frumpy in everything. She carefully unwrapped her present and lifted out a beautiful light blue and white, pin-striped shirt.

"It's perfect, Ben. Thank you," she said, with tears in her eyes.

By the time four o'clock came around, Jem was starting to look forward to her evening out with the girls, the first since having Tilly.

She heard the sound of a car tooting from outside.

"That will be them," Ben announced. "Are you ready?"

"As ready as I'll ever be," she replied, giving him a kiss before walking out of the door.

"What on earth are you lot up to?" she asked, climbing into Clare's Land Rover with the trailer hitched up behind it.

"We couldn't all fit in the horse lorry so Joe said we could borrow this," Suzie explained. "Now buckle up, it's time to go!"

"Jem, this is my friend Grace," Rose said, introducing her to the lady sitting next to Rose on the back seat.

"Hello Grace," Jem said, before turning her attention back to Suzie. "So where are we going?"

"A horse rescue centre. Doesn't it sound amazing!" replied Suzie.

"And we are taking the trailer because...?" Jem enquired.

"Just in case!" remarked Suzie.

Rose

Sitting in the back seat of the land rover trundling along the main road, heading for the rescue centre, Rose let her mind wonder to Andrew. He was about five foot ten, she thought. Being only five foot two herself, she struggled to gauge a man's height because they all looked tall to her. But whatever height he was, he was lovely. Slim, toned, with skew-whiff golden-brown hair that seemed to stick up in every direction, and a friendly warm smile. She had to admit it to herself, she was looking forward to seeing him again, just as much as she was looking forward to seeing the animals and learning about the centre.

She was pleased she had contacted Grace. She hadn't been sure if it was the right thing to do - it might have been too soon. But Grace had been delighted with her call, and with a very empty paddock to look at through her window, she happily agreed to accompany them on their rescue centre trip, just in case.

"We're here," Suzie announced, breaking her away from her thoughts. And then she spotted Andrew, opening the door to greet them.

Rose let the others go first, suddenly overcome with shyness at seeing him again. She stayed at the back to try and pull herself together.

"Hi Rose," Andrew said, taking her hand in his to greet her. Rose noticed that his hand was warm, and slightly rough. *No doubt from all the physical work he did with animals.*

"Follow me, ladies. Your tour starts this way."

After learning all about how the sanctuary was run and the relentless effort the team put in to rescue, rehabilitate and hopefully rehome the animals, Andrew announced it was time to meet some of the residents.

The ladies listened quietly as Andrew took them over to each animal, explaining the circumstances they had been found in, each more horrific than the last.

"And this little chap arrived this afternoon," Andrew announced.

"Oh my word," exclaimed Suzie. "It's a donkey! Oh, look at the dear little fellow, his feet look like Aladdin's slippers and he's as skinny as a rake. What's his name?"

"Mistletoe," Andrew said. "The girls on reception named him, and what with it being the first of December, they thought a donkey needed a Christmas name."

"Can I go in with him?" Suzie asked.

"Of course, he's super friendly," Andrew said, unlatching the stable door and letting her in.

Oh dear, Rose thought. *Methinks we will be going home with a donkey!* Rose turned to look for Grace, and suddenly noticed that she hadn't followed them all to meet Mistletoe. Working her way back through the animals she already met, she heard Grace's soft voice. "Well, aren't you just the most gorgeous little thing. Would you like a cuddle?"

Rose peeked over the stable doors until she found her. Grace was sitting on the straw bed that belonged to a palomino miniature Shetland mare.

"Isn't she beautiful?" Grace whispered, gently stroking the little pony's nose.

Rose was so transfixed, watching Grace bond with the little pony that she didn't notice Andrew come up behind her. Leaning around her, she could feel the warmth from his body and smell the subtle scent of his masculine aftershave, and she felt fizzing bubble up inside her.

"I see you have met Petunia," Andrew said. "She's looking for a new home, if you're interested?"

"Very much so," Grace replied, not taking her eyes off Petunia.

"Petunia was rescued two months ago; she looks very different to the neglected pony that was brought it. She's a seventeen-year-old pedigree miniature Shetland who has been ruthlessly used as a brood mare for her entire life. The paperwork shows she has produced fourteen foals. She was found in a terribly neglected state with her ten-month-old foal. We weaned him two weeks ago and found him a wonderful home three days ago."

"Maybe," Grace said tentatively, "Petunia could have a home with me?"

So that will be a donkey and a miniature Shetland coming home with us! Rose thought, chuckling to herself.

Paperwork completed, Mistletoe and Petunia were loaded in the horse box. A while later, they sat with takeaway fish and chips on their laps.

"We're taking the trailer just in case?" Jem said, between mouthfuls of delicious chips. "You sly old thing, Suzie. This was your plan all along, wasn't it? Animal mad, you are!"

All the ladies burst out laughing as the gang headed for home.

Riley

Riley was schooling Sundance for the sole reason of distracting herself and trying to calm her overactive mind. She and Molly had met their mother again, the week after Riley received her treasured pearl necklace. All had gone well, and with Nell giving her absolutely no excuse or reason to say no, she finally relented to Molly's persistent requests, and allowed her mother to pick Molly up from school and take her back to her flat for afternoon tea. Nell promised she would bring her home at five o'clock. It was now ten minutes to five.

No reason to stress about anything yet, Riley told herself, trying to quell the slowly rising panic. "Come on Sundance, it's all but dark now, time to finish and give you your supper," Riley said to the horse.

Riley had just begun to groom him down when she saw car lights heading up the drive. She checked her watch. It was two minutes to five. She breathed a huge sigh of relief. Her mother had not let her down.

"Hi Riley," Molly shouted, climbing out of the car. "Did you bring Pipsqueak in for me? I'll feed him now, I can't wait for Mum to meet him."

"Come on Mum!" Molly said, skipping over to the feed room to make up Pipsqueak's supper.

Nell cautiously ventured up to the yard to meet her daughters' horses.

"Hi, Mum, this is Sundance," Riley said, proudly introducing her horse.

"He's beautiful, Riley," her mum said, tentatively reaching out her hand to stroke his nose. Sundance turned his head and gently snuffled her hand, and Riley took that to mean that he liked her, or at least, was prepared to like her if she continued to be pleasant around him and do nothing to frighten him.

As always, Riley thought, *you always know what to do, Sundance. You always show me my own feelings, wise old man that you are.* She placed her hands under his mane and felt the heat of his body spreading through her fingers and warming them up from the chilly winter air.

"Over here, Mum, this is Pipsqueak's stable, come and meet him," Molly said, gesturing for her mother to follow her.

Nell had to lean over the stable door to see the little pony. "Ahhhhh, he's adorable, Molly!"

"And look, Mum, come and see who lives next door to Pipsqueak," Molly said, taking her mother by the hand and dragging her over to the neighboring stable. Peeking over the top of the stable she saw Mistletoe, "A donkey! Is he yours too, Molly?"

Giggling to her mother, Molly replied, "No, silly, only Pipsqueak is mine, he belongs to my friends, John and Joseph. He only arrived two weeks ago, he's a rescue donkey. Isn't he just the cutest thing ever? Well, apart from Pipsqueak, of course."

"He's gorgeous," her mother replied, smiling down at Molly.

Riley busied herself with Sundance's evening routine, but all the time listening intently to Molly and her mother's conversation. *They sound so normal,* she thought, *just like a regular family. You would never know what she used to be like. What she was like with me when I was Molly's age.* The mixed feelings swelled inside Riley as she struggled to forgive her mother, yet at the same time, she was genuinely pleased at the relationship she was slowly starting to build with Molly. *And me,* she thought ruefully, *if only I'd let her.*

After putting Sundance away in his stable for the night, she said to Molly, "It's time to go in for our dinner now. Say goodbye to Mum."

Riley watched Molly reach up and give her mother a goodbye hug. "See you soon, Mum," she said, and then scampered off into the house.

"Thank you so much for today, Riley, Molly and I had a wonderful time. Maybe next time you could join us?"

Riley could clearly see what an effort her mother was making for both her and Molly. She took a deep breath before speaking. "Hollybrook holds a Christmas Eve party every year. All the liveries and their families get together for a Christmas celebration. It's very low key, but maybe, would you like to come?"

Riley saw her mother's face break out into a beaming smile. "I would love to," she replied.

Riley nodded to acknowledge her acceptance. "I'll contact you soon with the details. I must go and get Molly's supper ready." Then she strode off to the house.

Andrew

Andrew was on his way to Hollybrook stables for his routine check on Mistletoe. His phone call with Suzie to arrange the visit two days ago left him buzzing with anticipation at the thought of seeing Rose again. He had been secretly hoping that he would bump into her during his visit.

"I'll let Rose know you're coming," Suzie had said. "She'll be thrilled to show off Winter and the progress she has made since your last visit." So, it now seemed guaranteed that he would see her.

Pulling into the car park, he saw Mistletoe and Winter tied up on the yard being pampered and fussed by Rose, Suzie and two boys. He climbed out of his car and strolled over to the happy little group. "Hi ladies," he said, then turned to the boys. "And who are you two?"

"I'm John," said the older of the boys. "And he's Joseph." He pointed at his brother.

"Mistletoe is ours," said Joseph, wrapping his arms around the little donkey.

"I can see you're taking great care of him," Andrew said kindly. "You're doing a fantastic job, boys." He was rewarded with two little faces beaming with pride under his praise.

And Andrew meant it. After two weeks under the care and attention of Suzie and her boys, he felt like he was looking at a different donkey.

"Joel has been to see him," John announced.

"Our farrier," Suzie explained.

"Look," said Joseph, pointing to Mistletoe's hooves. "He's coming out again next week."

The donkey's hooves had clearly been properly attended to by the farrier. They were not quite as they should be yet, but that was to be expected due to the level of his neglect. There was no doubt that there had been a huge improvement, enabling the donkey to finally be able to walk in comfort. The little fellow had also gained some weight. His skeletal body was not quite as bony as it was, and he just emanated a sense of being at peace, content with his new family. Andrew could not have been happier for the little donkey.

He turned his attention to Winter, who had now been in Rose's dedicated care for seven weeks. He was truly astounded at what she managed to achieve with the mare. Her body was finally starting to show the physique of what a flourishing horse should look like, flesh now padding out what used to be bare bones, and her bay coat sported a healthy shine. She looked wonderful.

"And look at Winter!" he exclaimed. "You have worked your magic with her Rose," he said, beaming at her.

"She's an absolute treasure," Rose replied, looking up into his eyes and smiling back.

Andrew felt himself glow whenever he was in Rose's company. There was just something about her that he found fascinating. He wanted to spend more time with her and get to know her better.

Out of the corner of his eye, he noticed Suzie looking at him, then Rose, then back at him. Embarrassed, he broke the spell he seemed to have been cast under and looked away from Rose, busying himself with Winter and stroking her neck.

"Hollybrook is having a Christmas party next week," Suzie announced. "All the liveries and their families get together for a festive knees-up on Christmas Eve. Do you want to come?" she asked. He could have sworn she slipped Rose a sly glance before swiftly turning her attention back to him, grinning from ear to ear.

Then Suzie turned to her boys. "Come on boys, let's take Mistletoe back out to Clarissa and Pandora's paddock." She rounded up the boys, then left Andrew and Rose standing somewhat awkwardly together on the yard.

In an attempt to fill the silence and find common ground, he blurted out, "I saw Grace and Petunia yesterday."

"I know, Grace told me," Rose replied. "She asked me to check her over before your visit. She was panicking that she might not be up to scratch as a rescue owner. You know she gives her bubble baths, warm water and everything!" Rose giggled. "And did you see the red lamp in her stable? It's to dry her off properly and keep her warm in this cold weather. Grace absolutely dotes on her; I'm so pleased they found each other."

Andrew laughed in response. "Yes, I noticed the heat lamp! And her wardrobe of brand-new rugs. She treats little Petunia like a queen, she's a very lucky pony. Petunia certainly landed on her feet with Grace as her new owner."

Rose nodded and smiled, then looking shyly up at him. "The party, the one Suzie mentioned, it's just a casual thing, food, music, drinks…lots of drinks," she said ruefully, grinning at him. "You would be welcome to come if you would like too?"

Andrew couldn't believe his luck. An evening spent with Rose? Wild horses wouldn't stop him from going. Aloud, in as steady a voice as he could muster, he replied, "Yes, I'd like to very much, thank you."

Suzie

Suzie woke on Christmas Eve morning overflowing with festive spirit. It was her first Christmas as Luke's wife and their first Christmas as a family, and she couldn't wait for the celebrations to begin.

She heard Luke calling, "Are you up yet Suze? You had better hurry up if you want to keep to your Christmas activity itinerary."

Jumping out of bed, she replied, "I'm on my way!"

Entering the kitchen, she saw John and Joseph sitting at the table munching on bacon sandwiches that Luke had just served up. He was wearing her bright red reindeer Christmas apron and reindeer antlers on his head.

She burst out laughing. "Eat up, boys!" she said. "The schedule says we need to be at the yard for ten o'clock sharp!" Then she tucked into her own delicious scrambled eggs on toast.

Arriving on the yard, Suzie noticed David and Ellen, who obviously had the same idea as her. They were just heading down the drive together with Captain and Jupiter for their own Christmas ride. The horses were decked out in red exercise sheets trimmed with white fur and reindeer antlers attached to their bridles. They all smiled and waved as they went past.

Gilly, Clarissa and Mistletoe were tied up on the yard being prepared for their Christmas outing. They had gold tinsel tied around their necks with jingle bells weaved through, red tinsel around their tales, and Santa hats on their heads to complete their attire. Suzie was adamant that the mini herd should not miss out on the spirit of Christmas.

"Ok, boys," Luke said. "Time to climb aboard your Christmas steeds!"

Joseph clambered up on Clarissa whilst Luke gave John a leg up on the enormous Gilly. "Are you ready, Suze?" he asked.

"We are," replied Suzie, proud as punch, standing next to the new addition, Mistletoe. Luke stepped out in front to head the little procession, then John and Gilly, with Joseph and Clarissa at their side, fell in step behind, leaving Suzie and Mistletoe to bring up the rear. They sang carols and Christmas songs with gusto, in time with the rhythmical beat of the jingle bells jingling with each of the horses' steps.

Suzie and the boys had always involved Clarissa in one way or another with their Christmas activities over the years, but today was by far the best Christmas Eve ride they had ever experienced. And little Mistletoe was there with them, the most Christmassy of all animals. Suzie's heart swelled with love and affection as she watched all of her boys enjoying themselves as a family, and the little donkey skipping along beside her just oozing Christmas spirit.

Arriving back on the yard, they found Molly waiting for them.

"Come on, boys, we have to put the tinsel up in the barn!" Molly said, then turned to Suzie. "Riley's already in the barn, she said to just come over when you've finished with the horses." Then she and the boys raced off to help prepare the barn for the party.

Suzie loved the preparations as much as the event itself, and for as long as Clarissa had lived at Hollybrook stables, she always helped Clare with the event they looked forward to all year, the Christmas Eve party.

Riley was taking her responsibilities very seriously. She was not going to let Clare down - the party was going to be perfect, and she was organizing everything with military precision. She sent Luke and David off to start the log burners. It would take hours to get the barn heated. Riley and Ellen were on twinkly light duty, and Suzie, as was her job every year, was in charge of creating the table decorations for the sprawling buffet and drinks tables. Joe had left early that morning to collect his mum and Matthew from the airport, but not before ticking off his job on Riley's list first - hooking up the music system. Jolly Christmas music was booming out of the speakers in the barn, creating a wonderfully festive atmosphere for the busy workers.

The afternoon flew by and after three hours of decorating it was time to go home and put their party clothes on.

"Luke," Suzie called out. "It's time to go, could you go and round up the boys please whilst I finish up my last job."

Pulling a fresh sprig of mistletoe out of her pocket, she hung it up on one of the exposed wooden beams of the barn. Looking up at it, she smiled slyly to herself. *Little flower of mischief and love,* she thought. *You might turn out to be very helpful for a certain vet and animal rescuer I know!*

She felt a tap on her shoulder and turned around to see who needed her attention. Facing Luke's chest, she slowly raised her eyes to meet his.

"We seem to be standing under mistletoe," he remarked, before scooping her up in his arms and planting a kiss firmly on her lips. "Ahhhh mistletoe! A man's best friend," he teased.

"A lady's best friend too!" she replied, giving him a peck on the cheek. "Now, enough tomfoolery! It's time to go home."

Jem

Jem woke for the first time in a very long time with a clear head. She waited momentarily for the cloud of gloom to engulf her, but the feeling of misery didn't arrive. Tentatively, she climbed out of bed and snuck into Tilly's room. Her gorgeous little girl was gurgling and cooing contentedly to herself. She crept over and peered into her cot. The baby girl noticed her mother, and Jem was met with a genuine smile lighting up her daughter's face.

"Good morning, beautiful girl," whispered Jem, gathering her up into her arms for a cuddle.

Jem padded downstairs, carrying Tilly, and that morning she saw her kitchen in a new light. Noah and Ben had spent hours decorating the house last week, and although she participated because she knew she had too, for Noah's sake, it had all been rather a chore. But this morning, she felt the warmth and cosiness the decorations brought to her home.

Was that a flutter of excitement I just felt? she thought, hardly daring to believe it. She made herself a cup of tea then settled on the sofa to nurse Tilly. Surprised and cautious, she thought, *Still no black cloud.* Suzie said her depression just upped and left like a puff of smoke one morning, never to be seen or felt again. *I wonder, could it be possible?* Jem wondered. Suzie always had a way of dispelling any unwanted emotions she might feel. Although Jem knew it was just a casual remark, what she'd said about her sadness vanishing like a puff of smoke, a typical Suzie statement, she knew that her friend was implying that over time, with the support of her family and friends, she would get better. *And maybe, oh how she hoped, that time was nearing.*

She checked the clock on the mantel piece nestled between the fresh green holly with bright red berries Noah had displayed on it. "They'll be home soon," Jem said to Tilly. "I think I'll set the table and make a start on breakfast."

Jem laid the red tablecloth on the table followed by their festive holly and ivy themed crockery, then settled Tilly in her bouncy chair and popped outside and snipped some fresh winter roses. Arranging them prettily in a vase, she stood back and admired her creation. She then found flour, eggs and milk and placed them on the kitchen counter. Turning to Tilly, she announced, "Pancakes for the boys when they come in!"

She heard the door open and Noah calling out, "Mum, we're home!"

"We're in the kitchen, breakfast is almost ready."

"Pancakes," Noah exclaimed. "Yummy."

Jem saw the surprise on Ben's face when he walked into the kitchen; a clean and tidy kitchen for starters, and a smiling Jem to boot. It wasn't what he had become used to over the past couple of months.

"Morning, Jem," he said, smiling at her. "Are you feeling better?" he asked, as he picked up Tilly for a morning cuddle.

Jem went over to him, still holding her wooden spoon, dripping pancake mixture across the floor as she went. "I think so. I think the cloud has gone, Ben. I haven't felt it all morning." Then she reached up on her tiptoes and kissed his cheek.

Settled around the thoughtfully decorated table, munching away on pancakes, Jem felt truly blessed to have her wonderful family, all cocooned in their cosy, festive home.

"How was Pandora? Everything ok?"

"All fine, I made up her feed whilst Ben took her rug off then we groomed her together," Noah explained. "She enjoyed the extra carrots we gave her."

"Thank you for taking such good care of her whilst I've been looking after Tilly. I think from tomorrow, Tilly and I will be able to join you with Pandora duties on a regular basis again," she said, smiling at them both.

The rest of Jem's day was spent hidden away upstairs wrapping Noah's and Tilly's presents that were bought in a daze over the past month. The wrapping was a job she had put off doing due to lack of motivation and energy, but it was a task she was now relishing, carefully wrapping each present in brown paper with different coloured ribbons. Tilly's presents were in gold ribbon, Noah's in green and Ben's were in red. She looked over the generous pile of presents in front of her, excitement for Christmas day with her family bubbling up inside her.

Ben knocked on their bedroom door. "Is it safe to come in?" he asked, peeking his head round.

Jem laughed. "Of course, come on in, everything is wrapped."

"So," said Ben, sitting on the bed next to her and the pile of presents. "Do you feel up to the Hollybrook Christmas party? I know you said you didn't feel like going this year but when I saw Riley at the yard this morning, she asked how you were and said if she change your mind then she would love for us all to join them. What do you think?"

Jem looked at Ben, her kind, lovely, thoughtful Ben. He had done so much for her over the past couple of months. He deserved a fun night out. *We all do,* she thought, breaking into a smile. "Yes, I think we should go," she said, then she leaned over and wrapped her arms around him, squeezing him tightly to her.

Returning her embrace, Ben whispered into her ear, "I've missed you Jem."

"I've missed you too, I'm back now," she replied, then she rested her head on his shoulder and closed her eyes. *Yes, I'm back,* she thought.

Rose

Rose was rudely woken at four o'clock in the morning by the shrill sound of her phone ringing. Mr Wilson, a local farmer, had a cow calving and she was showing signs of distress. He was phoning to ask Rose if she could come out to his farm and check on her.

Rose grumbled and groaned once she'd hung up the phone, knowing the icy coldness that awaited her as soon as she stepped outside of her warm little cottage.

"You enjoy your lie for the both of us," she told her cat, who was snuggled up between the folds of the duvet and showing no intention of leaving the comfy bed for hours. Rose bundled herself up into as many layers as she could, and with a flask of hot coffee in her hand, opened her door and headed out into the dark, cold, Christmas Eve morning.

On arriving at the farm, she was met with Buttercup nursing a fit and healthy calf. "You missed it all," Mr Wilson said ruefully. "So sorry to have woken you at such an ungodly hour. I really thought she was struggling, but as you can see, she managed all on her own in the end."

Rose watched Buttercup and her calf. She never tired of seeing such a natural, earthly sight as a new-born animal. "Always better to be on the safe side. You did the right thing to call me. Just look at them both together," she said, pointing at the nursing calf. "What a wonderful way to start the day, witnessing nature at its best." She smiled broadly at him. After Rose had checked mum and baby over, Mr Wilson invited her into his home where Mrs Wilson swiftly handed her a mug of hot chocolate and a plate piled high with hot buttered toast, laden with homemade apple and blackberry jam.

"We're so grateful to you, Rose," Mrs Wilson said. "Come in and warm yourself up in front of the fire."

It was still dark when she left the Wilson's farm, but feeling fully replenished after her generous breakfast, she decided to go to the yard, see Winter, complete her yard chores, then go home and back to bed for an hour. *It was supposed to be her day off, after all,* she thought with a wry smile.

Rose silently slid back the latch and let herself into Winter's stable and was welcomed by her gentle nicker. Slipping off her wet gloves, she slid her hands between Winter's rug and felt the warmth from her horse against her icy hands.

"Good morning, girl," she whispered, placing a kiss on her nose, then reluctantly removing her hands from her horsey radiator, "I'll be back in two ticks with your breakfast."

Rose loved the smell of Winter's morning mash, the sweet scent filling the arctic air as she mixed in the oil and cider vinegar that completed her feed.

"Here you go," she said, placing the bucket on the floor in Winter's stable, then listened to Winter greedily gobble up her breakfast.

"Guess who I'm seeing today? Andrew! He's coming to the party this evening. I really like him," Rose confided to her horse. "You like him too, don't you? I can't wait to wear my new dress. As soon as Ellen found out Andrew was coming to the party, she dragged me out shopping to buy a new dress. I've got to admit though, I'm pleased she did. She helped me find the perfect dress. It's bright red, long sleeved, knee length and made from wool. We both agreed that a party in a barn in the middle of winter would definitely warrant a woollen dress! I also got some black tights to pair with it and I'm thinking my kitten heel black boots should finish the outfit," Rose explained.

Rose lent against Winter, closed her eyes and pictured Andrew. *He's so handsome, and he has such a natural way with animals. He seemed pleased when I invited him to the party, I hope he's looking forward to seeing me as much as I am to see him!* Rose thought dreamily. *I wonder if he will ask me out on a date! I reckon that will be the way to tell if he actually likes me. If he asks me out on a date at the party then I'll know he likes me for me, rather than just as a work colleague.*

"Morning Rose," Riley said, bringing Rose back to reality. "You're here early."

"Emergency call out at four am," Rose explained to her. "So I thought I'd come and feed Winter before going back to bed to catch up on some sleep!"

Riley laughed. "Definitely, you'll need your energy for the party tonight, I'll see you later." Then she strode off to start her own morning yard chores.

Saying her goodbyes to Winter, Rose found just enough energy to drive her car home, then climb up the stairs before collapsing into bed.

Rose woke, for the second time that day, and her cat was gently patting her face with his paw. She slowly opened her eyes and saw that it was dark outside. In her sleepy slumber she said, "Arghhh it's still night time, I'll get up and feed you as soon as the sun rises." Then she snuggled back under the duvet and closed her eyes.

She jumped up with a jolt. "Oh my word, I've slept all day, what time is it?" Her cat looked at her in a haughty manner. "No wonder you're cross, you must be starving," she said, climbing out of bed and heading downstairs to feed her hungry cat. She looked at her watch. Six o'clock. *Oh no,* she thought, racing back up the stairs and jumping in the shower.

Riley

Riley watched Molly twirling in circles around her, showing off her new, bright pink, fairy princess style party dress. Ever since she turned the calendar over from November to December, her whole focus had been organising and preparing for the party. Clare's parties were legendary, and she did not want to let her down, and being so focused on the party itself, it wasn't until last week, when Molly and Joe came in carrying two glossy carrier bags that it dawned on her that she and Molly didn't have anything to wear. They spent their lives in jeans or jodhpurs and their wardrobes were woefully lacking anything suitable for a party.

"What have you got there?" she asked Molly.

"A party dress! Joe took me shopping after school. He got one for you too," Molly replied, grinning from ear to ear. "Go on Joe, show her the dress," Molly said, hopping from foot to foot with excitement.

Joe handed over one of the glossy bags to Molly, and the other to Riley. "This one is for you, I hope you like it," he said, smiling shyly at her.

Opening the bag, Riley slowly lifted out a forest green, long sleeved, figure-hugging, floor-length dress, with specks of gold woven through it. Riley was lost for words, spell bound with the elegance of the dress she was holding in her hands.

"Oh Joe, it's absolutely beautiful, thank you so much," she gushed, stretching her hand out to take hold of his and squeezing it affectionately.

"After all the hard work you have put into get this party ready, we thought you deserved a treat, didn't we Molly?"

"We did," Molly replied proudly.

Riley looked at herself in the mirror. She hardly recognized herself in the mystical dress, her auburn hair piled up on top of her head, showing off the scooped neckline. She felt tingles run through her at Joe's kindness. *I'm so lucky to have him,* she thought.

Riley heard the doorbell ring. "Come on, Molls, save some twirling for the dance floor! It sounds like our first guest has arrived."

Skipping down the stairs, Riley and Molly rushed to their front door to welcome their first guest.

"Mum!" shrieked Molly in delight as she launched herself at her mother. "Come on, the party is about to start, let's go over to the barn."

"Hi Mum," Riley said. "You look nice." She meant it, too. Nell had obviously made an effort for the party. She was wearing a charcoal grey dress, black tights, black boots, and an intricately designed holly and ivy festive scarf.

"Oh Riley, you look absolutely wonderful, that dress is gorgeous," her mother complimented her.

Glowing under her mother's praise, she replied, "Joe gave it to me." Smiling at her mum, she said, "Now let's go over to the barn and get this party started!"

By seven o'clock the party was in full swing, and Riley had just received a message that Joe, Clare and Matthew would be arriving in ten minutes. Continuing her hostess duties, Riley grabbed another bottle of wine and set about topping everyone's drinks up. On reaching David, Ellen and Andrew, Ellen turned to her.

"Have you seen Rose?" Ellen asked. "No one seems to have seen or heard from her all day. I thought she would have been here by now?"

"Not since six thirty this morning," Riley replied. "Emergency call out," she explained. "All turned out fine in the end, and she definitely said she was coming."

Then, as if on cue, Rose came tumbling through the door. "I'm so sorry I'm late. Has Clare arrived yet? Have you guys seen outside? It's snowing!"

Everyone gathered around the door to see the first flurry of snow, then the headlights of a car heading up the drive penetrated through the wintery scene, lighting up the delicate snowflakes dancing in the wintery night sky.

Clare

Clare couldn't believe it when she and Matthew stepped through the arrivals door at the airport and found Joe waiting for them.

"Joe, you're here! What a surprise," she said, opening her arms to embrace her son. "We told you we'd get a taxi, we didn't want to put you out. We know how busy you have been getting the party organised."

"Riley is holding the fort, she insisted I come and collect you," he replied, bending down to receive his mother's hug. Then, holding out his hand, he greeted Matthew with a firm handshake. "Welcome home."

The long car journey home was filled with excited chatter as they caught up with each other's news.

"I can't wait to meet Winter and Mistletoe, and did I tell you? I have a new horse coming in for training the first week of January," Clare told Joe.

Clare's breath caught in her throat when they finally turned into Hollybrook stables driveway. *Home,* she thought. *How wonderful to be home.*

Clare had experienced a trip of a lifetime with Matthew. Florence was without a doubt one of the most beautiful cities she had ever been privileged enough to visit, and the Italian food was absolutely sublime. The different cultures, architecture, cuisine and horses all made for a truly wonderful experience. She and Matthew had enjoyed the most fantastic time together, and she would definitely accompany him on many more work trips abroad, but never again for such a lengthy time. Two months was a long time and Clare was ready to come home. As they approached Hollybrook, a layer of snow settled on the ground and snowflakes fluttering in the sky made her home look like a winter wonderland.

"They're here!"

"They've arrived!"

"Welcome home!"

Clare heard her friends call out to them as soon as she climbed out of the car.

"Come in out of the cold," Riley said, ushering them into the festively decorated barn.

Clare felt like she was stepping into a magical Christmas world when she set foot inside. "Oh Riley, you have well and truly outdone yourself, everywhere looks amazing," Clare exclaimed, taking in the hundreds of twinkly lights, the boughs of red berried holly adorning the tables, and red and gold tinsel hanging from beam to beam, sparking against the twinkle lights. And the small log burners, one on each corner of the barn, were emitting much needed heat and casting a warm glow over the barn, creating an enchanting atmosphere. And the crowning glory was an eight-foot Christmas tree towering above everyone, standing proud, centred at the back end of the barn. A large red sparkly star was sitting on the top, red and gold baubles hanging from the ginormous tree's branches, and more twinkly lights.

Oh, you can never have too many twinkly lights at Christmas time, Clare thought, taking in the perfect Christmas scene before her.

And then to her great surprise, little John and Joseph jostled through the door with the most adorable looking donkey.

"Mistletoe," Clare exclaimed in delight. "I've heard so much about you, welcome to Hollybrook stables! And what perfect timing for your arrival, you are the perfect addition to any Christmas party."

Clare watched everyone fuss over the little donkey, before Suzie told the boys it was time to put him to bed. She didn't want him to get overwhelmed at his first Christmas party!

"Pleased to be home?" Matthew asked, sidling up beside her and offering her a glass of wine.

Taking a sip of sparkling fizz, she felt the bubbles bouncing on her tongue as she stood back and watched her family and friends enjoying themselves.

Molly, John, Joseph and Noah were all laughing and giggling together on the dance floor, taking it in turns to spin each other round and round...and then let go. Clare stifled a chuckle when she saw Noah spin wildly into John, causing them to both topple over in shrieks of laughter.

Jem and Ben were taking a rest from dancing, baby Tilly cradled in Jem's arms. Ben was sitting tall and proud of his little family, with one arm casually draped around Jem, both of them watching the antics that the children were getting up to and giggling between themselves.

Suzie and Luke were animatedly chatting with David and Ellen, happy smiles on all of their faces, and then she heard them all burst into laughter at something Suzie said.

And that must be Andrew, she thought, noticing a friendly looking man, quietly chatting with Rose. From Clare's position, Andrew and Rose didn't know they could be seen, and she watched Andrew look up and point to Rose when he realised they were standing underneath the mistletoe. Clare watched him smile down at Rose. He slowly reached his hand up and gently traced his finger down her cheek. Leaning forward...

Yikes, thought Clare, turning away. *Absolutely not for me to watching!* She was secretly pleased that Rose had finally found someone, though. *And a very handsome someone too,* Clare noted.

Then she spotted Riley and Joe chatting to Nell. Clare couldn't believe the difference in the kind looking lady, who was smiling and laughing, standing next to Riley, compared with the train wreck of a woman who had turned up on her doorstep last year. Clare was absolutely thrilled for the girls that their mother had got her act together and was finally starting to behave like the mother they deserved.

And look at Riley in that dress, Clare mused, so proud of the young woman she had become. What a handsome couple they made, Riley in her elegant dress and Joe in his smart shirt and immaculate black jeans.

Clare felt immense gratitude for each and every person in her barn that evening, all her family and friends. She felt a sense of absolute fulfilment in her life. She leant back against Matthew's chest and rested her head on his shoulder.

"Absolutely," she replied. "There's no place like home."

Printed in Great Britain
by Amazon